A **SporTellers**™ Book

RACE TO WIN

EVE COWEN

A PACEMAKER® BOOK

Fearon / Janus
Belmont, California

Simon & Schuster
Supplementary Education Group

SporTellers™

Catch the Sun
Fear on Ice
Foul Play
High Escape
Play-Off
Race to Win
Strike Two
Stroke of Luck

Senior development editor: Christopher Ransom Miller
Content editor: Carol B. Whiteley
Production editor: Mary McClellan
Design manager: Eleanor Mennick
Illustrator: Bob Haydock
Cover: Bob Haydock

ISBN 0–8224–6479–9

Library of Congress Catalog Card Number: 80–82988

Printed in the United States of America.

1. 9 8 7 6 5

Contents

In the Pit 1

Tina DeVita and Lou Amber.

The voice over the loudspeaker spoke two names and then stopped for a second. Then it went on as two cars rolled to a stop in the warm-up area.

The cars for the next race are lining up. That's Tina DeVita in the '74 Monza. It's only her second year in pro gas racing, but she has been moving up fast. DeVita comes from Highland, Texas—the same town where the great driver Roy Cooke lives.

Tina began spinning her wheels in the warm-up area. As they spun in the water there, the wheels got hot. The noise of her engine was so loud that the words being said over the loudspeaker about Lou Amber were lost to her ears. It didn't matter. Lou Amber was only a name to her—a name and a '74 Pinto. What mattered was that Tina had to beat Lou Amber and his car in a race down a straight quarter-mile course. And if she beat Amber, she would have to race against another driver—and another, and another. Until she made it to the last race. And that, she knew, would be against Roy Cooke.

She hoped her luck would hold out.

As she spun her wheels, the tires grew hot. This would give her better traction at the start of the race. Tina listened to the sound of her engine. Something was wrong. The engine seemed a little sluggish. Tina shook her head.

"Oh, great," she said to herself. It was only Tina's third race of the day. There were a lot more runs the yellow Monza would have to make. Too late to do anything about it now, Tina thought. I'll have to check it out later.

When the sign was given, Tina and Lou Amber drove their cars to the starting line. The crowd in the hot, late-morning sun watched and talked as both drivers made try-out starts and then backed up to the line.

When the cars were ready to go, the crowd grew still.

Tina felt as she always did just before a race was about to start. She felt she was a part of the car—that she and the car moved as one. All she thought about was hitting the gas just as the last light on the pole turned to green.

Eyes on the lights, Tina waited. Suddenly the last light went from yellow to green. She hit the gas. But the car didn't jump forward as fast as it should have. The engine missed as the Monza speeded down the track. Something was really wrong.

Lou Amber was in the lead by the time the Monza started to straighten out. Tina saw him off her left front wheel. But halfway down the course, Amber had trouble of his own. The Pinto was losing oil. Tina passed it and finished in front.

After her Monza crossed the line, Tina braked and looked back. Amber's car had left a trail of oil behind it. Tina watched as the Pinto turned and moved slowly toward the pits. As she headed for the pits in her own car, she shook her head. She had won the race. But if the Pinto hadn't given out, she might not have.

Tina worried about her car. But she worried about something else too. Angie—her sister. Angie would throw a fit when she heard the Monza's engine had missed. She would be angry because Tina had come close to losing the race. Angie thought of herself as the best mechanic around.

When Tina pulled into the pit, Angie was waiting for her. And there was a dark, angry look on her face. But there were other people waiting for Tina too. Her mother and her father. And Mark, Joey, and Timmy, her younger brothers. There were also 10 or 12 people she didn't know. During National Hot Rod Association races, fans could buy pit passes to visit the drivers.

Tina took off her helmet and wiped her hot face. Angie came up to her. In an angry voice she said, "What happened out there? What are you, a Sunday driver?"

"The car—" Tina started to say.

"Don't tell me something went wrong with the car," Angie broke in. "I don't want to hear it."

Everyone in the pit watched the two sisters.

"Let me finish," Tina went on. "I could tell something was wrong in the warm-up area. The engine was sluggish. Then it started to miss at the starting line. Better take a look at it, OK?"

Angie lifted the hood. The whole DeVita family crowded around the car. They all began talking at once. The fans behind them started talking and pointing too.

"Pipe down, everyone," Angie suddenly shouted. "A person can't think in this noise."

The talking stopped right away. Everyone in the DeVita family knew that Angie was boss in the pit. And the fans decided they had better listen to her too.

"Now," Angie said. "That's better." She looked under the hood.

Tina watched as Angie looked the engine over carefully. "Could it be the fuel?" Tina asked at last. "That might be what made the engine miss."

"I can't see anything else wrong," Angie said as she straightened up. "It's the fuel, all right. And that means we have to empty the tank and start all over." She wiped her hands on a rag as she spoke. "Heads are going to roll for this. We paid a lot of money for special fuel. And it's dirty." She laughed, but it was an angry laugh. "Dirty fuel. Someone is going to hear from me about it."

"Take it easy," said Tina. "These things can happen."

"Well, they shouldn't," said Angie. She stormed out of the pit.

Mr. DeVita took a few steps back from the car and shook his head. *"Drag racing,"* he said as Angie left. The way he said it told Tina and Angie they were out of their minds. They had heard him sound that way before. Mr. DeVita thought that if Tina and Angie had any sense, they would get out of drag racing for good. And come back to Highland, Texas, to work in the family flower shop. It was an old story. And it was always told in the same way and in the same voice—*"Drag racing."*

"Oh, Pop," Tina said. It was what she always said when her father let her know he didn't like racing. It said: Let's not go into it again. This is the way Angie and I want to live. This is the way it's going to be.

Her mother came over to her and put an arm around her. "Don't worry about anything," Mrs. DeVita told her. "It's what you want to do. So do it. And if you need some money to work on the car, I have a little put away."

Tina smiled. "Thanks, Mom. We're OK for now. As long as nothing else goes wrong. Besides, I know what your plans are for that money you're saving. You're going to fly to Italy to visit your family. So keep your money. And with any luck, Angie and I will win some more to help you get there."

Tina was glad that her mother stood behind her in her racing. But sometimes Tina felt the same way her father felt about the sport. Drag racing in the pros was hard work. Tina was often up against drivers who had been at it a long time. They had more money behind them. And she was finding out that things could go wrong any time they wanted to.

As Tina stood there thinking, Angie came storming back into the pit. She looked at her family. Then she looked at the fans. "There's no one to tell off," she said, still angry. "At least not yet. I checked with all the other mechanics. And we all got the same fuel from the same place. No one had trouble with the fuel but us. That means only one thing could have happened."

Angie looked hard at Tina. "Someone fooled around with our fuel tank today. Someone who doesn't want you to win the NHRA U.S. Nationals."

Win or Lose **2**

The next day, as Tina waited in the pits for the race to begin, a big man with gray hair and a ready grin walked up to her.

He flashed her a wide smile. "Nice day for a race," he said in his deep, warm voice. The man was Roy Cooke, the driver she needed to beat in that meet, the U.S. Nationals.

"So it is," Tina said, returning the smile. Inside, though, she felt as if a storm were coming up—a storm made by Angie. Her sister believed that Roy Cooke had added something to their Monza's fuel in yesterday's race to keep him from losing to Tina. It was a good thing Angie had left the pit for a minute. Or she'd be taking on Cooke right then.

Tina was angry, too, to think that someone had fooled with the tank. But the fuel was OK today. And she was sure that Roy Cooke hadn't fooled with it. Roy had been her driving teacher in Highland, Texas. He had helped her make it to where she was now. He had helped Angie too. Tina's mechanic sister had learned how to pull a car to pieces in Cooke's Speed Shop. And then how to put it back together again.

Cooke was also Mr. DeVita's best friend. Tina often thought that her father didn't like racing because he knew that one day Tina and Roy Cooke would have to fight it out on the quarter-mile track.

Tina hated to be the one to beat Roy Cooke in pro gas drag racing. He had helped her so much. And she didn't like the idea of paying him back by beating him. There could only be one winner, though. And she wanted to win. She had worked hard for it.

Roy Cooke headed back to his car as Tina put on her helmet. Cooke drove a '74 Monza just like Tina's. And like Tina, he had a top mechanic. The man's name was Gil Hughes. Hughes was a tall, thin man who never said much. But if there was something wrong with a car, he could find it. Angie had said that he was the best in the business—next to her.

Tina got in her car as Angie came back to the pit. Angie looked happy, and she gave Tina a good luck tap on the roof. Tina started the engine and nosed her Monza toward the warm-up area. Cooke pulled out of the pits and started to roll along right next to her. He turned and waved at her. She waved back. She knew Cooke was trying to make her remember that it was only a race. No matter who lost, it would not be the end of the world.

That was true. Tina had raced against Roy Cooke in seven big meets before. She had won some and lost some. And it hadn't been the end of the world when she had lost. There were many meets before the World Finals. And the winner of each one made points. It was the number of points all put together that would decide who would race in the finals.

Right now she and Roy Cooke were dead even in the points game. If Tina won the U.S. Nationals, she would be in front. But if she lost, there was still one more elimination race to be held in Seattle before the World Finals.

It was called the Fallnationals. If she lost to
Roy Cooke today, she could still catch up in
points at the Fallnationals.

Both Monzas moved slowly up to the starting line, and the fans got ready for the big
race of the day. Tina and Roy each made a
tryout start and backed up. Then they waited,
ready to move out fast.

Tina's eyes were fixed on the starting
lights. Suddenly the yellow light was gone
and the green was bright. Tina didn't waste
even a quarter of a second. She hit the gas
pedal. Her front wheels were high in the air
when the trouble came. Her back wheels dug
in. The car slid to the right. As her front
wheels came down, Tina set the Monza on a
straight course. But it was too late. Cooke had
shot down the course without a problem. The
race was his.

"What went wrong?" Tina wondered out
loud as she drove slowly back to the pits. The
rear tires must have been low on air. But that
was the last thing Angie checked before the
race.

"Trying to teach the Monza how to dance?"

Tina heard Angie's cutting line as she
climbed out of the car. Then Mrs. DeVita ran

over to Tina. "I thought for a minute you were out of control," she said.

"I'm OK," Tina said. "But the tires aren't. You should have been more careful when you checked the air, Angie."

"Are you trying to teach me my job? Those tires were just right," Angie fired back. "Maybe you ran over something sharp on your way to the warm-up area. Or maybe something happened while you were talking to Roy Cooke. I saw you together as I walked back to the pits before the race. Maybe *he* let some air out of your tires."

"You're out of your mind, Angie. Nothing like that went on. Check the tires over and find out what really happened. Don't give me a hard time. I just lost the U.S. Nationals."

"I will," Angie said. "I'll check every square inch of those tires. And if I find any sign that someone fooled with them, that someone better watch out."

CHAPTER 3

Highland Blues

"Oh, no! Say it isn't so!"

The words rang out from under the yellow Monza. The car was parked in the DeVitas' garage. The voice belonged to Angie. She had been checking over the Monza all morning.

"What's the matter now?" Tina had been reading on a chair next to the Monza. She looked up when Angie spoke.

"The torque converter." Angie rolled out from under the car. There was oil on her face and hands.

"Don't tell me," Tina said. "I don't want to know."

"You have to know. The torque converter isn't working right," said Angie. "We may have to get a new one."

"We can't," Tina said, jumping up. "There isn't time. We're leaving for the Fallnationals in eight days. And the only place that makes the kind of converter we need is the LBH Company. . .in California."

"Then we'll have to tell them to send us one right away." Angie wiped her hands on a rag and started to pick up the telephone.

"You forgot something, Angie."

Angie looked up. "What is that?"

"Money," said Tina. "We don't have the money we need to buy a new converter."

Angie shook her head. "That's something *I* don't want to know. You'll just have to find the money. If you want to race in the Fall-nationals, you are going to need a new torque converter."

Tina walked out of the garage and into the DeVita house. She knew enough not to say another word to her sister. It was hard enough to talk to Angie when things were going well. When things were bad, it was like talking to a stone wall.

And Tina knew Angie was right. Tina would have to raise the money. There was only one way to do that. She had to find another sponsor. Tina sat down and picked up the telephone. She called everyone she could think of who might be able to put up some money. But after an hour, it looked as if almost all the sponsors were on vacation. The few people she spoke to were suddenly short of money.

Tina put the telephone down with a bang. Sponsors! They were all alike. When you didn't need them, they were around. But when you wanted them—nothing. With a shake of her head, she walked the few blocks to her father's flower shop. She thought working with him would help her forget her troubles.

"What's the matter? You look like you lost your best friend," her father said as she walked in.

"Only my best torque converter. Angie said we have to have a new one," Tina told him. She looked sadly down at some beautiful roses.

"Drag racing," her father said in that special voice. He turned away.

"Why not give your daughter the money?" said a voice from the front of the flower shop. But Mr. DeVita had already gone into the back room.

Tina looked up when she heard the voice. Roy Cooke had come into the shop and was standing by the front door. Gil Hughes was with him. "Thanks for saying that," Tina laughed as she waved hello. "But it's no use asking him. He's still hoping I'll get out of drag racing."

"Tell you what," Cooke went on. "I'll let you have the money—all you have to do is give

Cooke's Speed Shop publicity on your car."

Hughes put his hand on Roy's arm. He said, "You must be kidding, Roy."

Cooke laughed. "I am kidding. It's not a bad idea, though."

"The fans would love it," Tina said, laughing again. "But I don't think Angie would go for it at all."

"I hear Angie has been telling people some interesting things," Gil Hughes said with an angry look on his face. "I hear she's telling people that she thinks Roy is trying to get you out of the race."

Tina shook her head. "She's just mad about all the things that have been happening to our car. She doesn't really think Roy had anything to do with them."

Cooke smiled. "If she does believe I fooled with your car—well, then you should let me pay for your new torque converter. That will show her that I'm not trying to keep you from racing. And you can pay me back with your winnings."

"OK," Tina said. "You're on. I'll take the money from you. And I *will* pay you back with my winnings."

Roy and Tina laughed as they shook hands. But Tina was worried as well as happy. There was no way she could tell Angie where the money had come from.

* * *

"Oh, torque converter, where are you?" Angie asked as she and Tina sat under the lights in the DeVita garage. "It should have been here by now," she said, hitting at a fly. "A week is more than enough time for a converter to come from California to Texas."

"I'm worried too," said Tina. "LBH said they would send it by World Parcel Service. That shouldn't have taken this long."

"Let's call LBH and find out what's going on," Angie said.

Tina thought that was a good idea and told Angie she would make the call. She headed for the house and the telephone. But LBH had bad news for her. She walked slowly back to the garage to tell it to Angie.

"They sent us the torque converter a week ago—the day you called."

"OK," said Angie. "Then where is it?"

"They said it came here to the house and that you signed your name to the ticket."

"I what?" Angie's face turned red.

"Take it easy," said Tina. "I told them to check into it. That you never signed your name to any ticket."

Angie's face was deep red now. "I can't believe this," she said.

"I can't either," Tina told her. She sat down. "But we have to think about what we are going to do now. We have to leave for Seattle tomorrow. And we don't have a new torque converter. We'll have to go to Seattle by way of California to pick one up. It's easy enough to drive there. But LBH won't give us a new converter until we get the signed ticket for the old one from World Parcel Service and show them that you never signed it. Not unless we pay them for another one. All that will take much too much time."

"This can't be happening to us," Angie said as she hit the back of a chair.

"Oh, I'm sick of the whole thing," Tina said suddenly. "Let's just go to Seattle. Forget the new converter. I'll run the race with things as they are." Tina turned and left the garage. She didn't want to hear what Angie had to say.

But Angie didn't have anything to say. She never brought up the torque converter again. And the next day as the family packed to head for Seattle, Angie couldn't stop smiling.

When the whole family was ready to go, Tina, Angie, and Timmy got into the front seat of the truck that carried the Monza. Mr. and Mrs. DeVita and the two older boys piled into their big Pontiac. But Angie would not let Tina drive.

"You have a good rest," she said. "I'll drive."

"OK," Tina said. "I'll drive later."

"Forget it," said Angie. "I know we always take turns. But on this trip I'll do it all. You just sit back and take it easy. We want you to be rested for the Fallnationals."

Tina didn't know what to make of it. But she did know one thing. What Angie wanted, Angie got.

"OK," Tina said. "Give me the maps then. I'll let you know when to change roads."

"Not this time, Tina," Timmy said. "*I'm* reading the maps. Angie said it was a good thing for me to learn."

Tina just shook her head. "I'm being treated like a queen," she said. Then she smiled. It felt good for a change to have other people do all the work.

After many hours of watching oil wells, shopping centers, and miles of open country move past her window, Tina fell asleep. When she woke up, it was late afternoon. She looked out the front window. The sinking sun beat down on the hood of the truck and made it shine.

"We stop soon," Angie said. As she spoke, she made a sharp left turn onto a new road.

"Wait a minute," said Tina. "Didn't you just make a wrong turn?"

"Go back to sleep," said Angie. "I told you I'm doing the driving."

"But this isn't the way to Seattle," Tina said.

"That's right," said Angie. "We're going to California to get a torque converter. I have enough money to buy another one."

"But where did you. . . ?" Suddenly Tina got angry. "OK, Angie. You have Mom's money. Well, we're not going to use it. No torque converter is worth her trip to Italy. Now turn around and get back on the road for Seattle. Or I won't drive in that race."

CHAPTER 4

The Road West

"Wild West Motel. Sounds good to me," said Angie as a small motel came into sight. "Let's stop here for the night." She waved to the Pontiac behind her and then pointed at the motel. The big car followed Angie into the motel parking lot. In a minute all the DeVitas were standing together and talking.

"OK," Tina broke in. "Hold it. I have a question. Are you all in on this together?"

"What are you talking about?" It was Mr. DeVita who spoke.

"You know just what I'm talking about," Tina answered. "How could you, Pop? How can you let Mom spend her money this way?"

"Take it easy," Mr. DeVita said. "Just take it easy. You know you'll get your money back from LBH when they see that Angie never signed for the converter. When you get the money from them, you'll be able to pay your mother back. There's nothing to worry about."

"I should think you wouldn't want me to get a new converter," Tina told him. "You have never liked my racing. And a new converter will just help me to race more."

"I heard that you owe Roy Cooke money for the torque converter that never came. I want you to be able to race so you can win and pay him back." Mr. DeVita looked at her, hard. "I don't know why you took the money from Roy," he said. "I could have gone to the bank and taken the money out for you."

"But I couldn't have asked you," Tina said. "Not when I know you don't want me to race."

"Maybe you couldn't," Mr. DeVita said. "But this is just why I didn't want you racing. I knew this kind of thing could happen. Now you owe Roy Cooke money, and you're going to race against him as well."

"OK, OK," said Tina. "I guess I'm in over my head. But it's my head—not Mom's. I'm not taking Mom's money. And that's the end of it." As she turned to walk toward the motel office, she looked at Angie. "Mom's money, Angie. How could you?"

Just then, Mrs. DeVita broke in. "That's enough. I'm tired of all this fighting. It's my money. So I'm the one to say how it will be spent. And I say I want to spend it on a new torque converter. Now, let's all go and check in. And then have some dinner and get to bed. We have a long way to drive tomorrow."

* * *

It was four o'clock in the morning. Tina awoke with a start. She sat up and listened. Then she whispered across the room, "Did you hear something, Angie?"

"What?" Angie was only half awake.

Tina listened again, but she heard nothing. "Something woke me. I wonder if someone was fooling with the truck. Did you check it before we got in bed?"

"What do you mean, did I check it?"

"Did you check the lock?"

"Of course I did," said Angie. "Would I forget something like that?"

"I thought I heard the Monza engine," said Tina.

She and Angie listened again, but all they heard was the room fan.

"You were dreaming," Angie said. "Go back to sleep."

*   *   *

A knock at the door woke Tina and Angie the first thing in the morning. It was their brother Timmy. "OK," he said. "Where did you hide the Monza?"

"What are you talking about?" Angie looked up as she closed the top of her bag.

"Just what I said. Where did you hide the Monza?"

"Where I always hide it," said Angie. "On the truck. Where do you think?"

"It's not there."

"What?" Angie's face turned white. So did Tina's. In a second they were out the door and standing next to the truck. The Monza was gone.

No one spoke. Then Tina cried, "I knew it! That noise! I did hear something last night."

Angie pulled Tina behind her to the truck. "Come on," she said. "It can't be far. There wasn't much gas in the tank."

The rest of the family got into the Pontiac. Soon Mr. DeVita found the Monza parked on a side street. He started honking his horn. People on the street came walking over to see what was happening. By the time Angie and Tina got there with the truck, a crowd stood around the Monza.

"Someone get the police," Tina said.

Just then a man pulled up in a black and white car. He stepped out of it. "I'm Officer Lopez," he said. "What's the problem?"

"Our race car," said Tina. "It was dragged off our truck last night and taken for a joy ride."

The police officer looked at Tina. "You're not from around here, are you?"

"We're on our way to California," Tina said. "About four in the morning they must have picked the lock on our truck. Then they must have rolled the Monza off and jumped the wires to start it."

Angie was looking the Monza over as Tina talked. "The wheels," she said at last. "The wheels are out of line. And the tie rod is bent. That means we will probably have to buy a new rod. And stop at a garage to have it fixed.

That means we'll waste time looking for a shop that can handle it. And we'll need more money."

Angie looked hard at the police officer. "I hope you find the kids who did this," she said. "Because if you don't, I will. And I'll see that they pay for this."

The police officer smiled a small smile. "Better cool off now," he said to Angie. "All I have is your word for what happened. For all I know, *you* stole that car. And dragged it here last night."

"Oh, come on," said Angie. "Don't you know who that woman is?" She pointed to Tina and waited for an answer that wasn't coming. "That's Tina DeVita," Angie said at last. "She's going to win the NHRA World Finals in pro gas drag racing. And I'm her sister. I own that car with her. So why would I steal something I already own?"

"Never heard of any Tina DeVita," said the police officer. "Only pro gas racer I know is Roy Cooke, the man staying at the Desert Motel over on the other side of town."

CHAPTER 5

The Race Is On

"I knew it," Angie cried. "He's behind this. Roy Cooke. Roy *Crook* is more like it!"

"Take it easy," Mr. DeVita said. "Those are strong words. Roy is a good friend of mine. He may want to win. But I know he wouldn't want to hurt Tina."

"Oh, let's get out of here," said Angie. "I'll get the truck. The papers that say we own the Monza are in it. We can show them to this police officer. And then we can get out of here. Remember something, though." She looked at her father. "Two can play at this game."

Angie started to walk up the street, but in a second she stopped dead. The truck was coming slowly toward her. Behind the wheel was Mrs. DeVita.

In a moment, Mrs. DeVita pulled up next to the Monza. "Get a move on. All of you," she called. "I'm the driver now. And here's what we're going to do. We're going to Los Angeles. First we'll get the torque converter from LBH. Then we'll have the tie rod fixed and go on to Seattle. The Fallnationals won't wait for anyone, you know." Mrs. DeVita gunned the engine to show her family she wasn't kidding. "Now I don't want to hear another word from any of you. Right now, I'm the boss."

* * *

The Monza had been fitted with a new torque converter. Its wheels had been lined up. And the whole family had made it to Seattle without another fight. They had been in time for the start of the meet.

Angie was pleased with the way Tina had sailed through her elimination races. But Angie wasn't happy that Roy Cooke had done the same thing. Now it was between Tina and Roy. She just hoped Tina could win.

Then it was Sunday, the big day. The weather was clear and dry. And Tina's Monza was in top shape. Angie decided to see if Cooke's Monza was in shape too.

Angie found Tina on her return from Cooke's pit. "His car looks good," Angie said. "But I can tell you Cooke is worried. He knows what he did to our car in that horse town didn't stop us. And he knows we mean to win. Remember, Tina. You're younger than he is. You can act faster. You can win on the yellow light. Just be ready to flash out off of the starting line before Roy."

"I get the point, Angie," said Tina. "You don't have to worry about me. I can handle it."

Tina didn't want to think too much about Roy Cooke. He was just another driver, she tried to tell herself. She wanted to win the race. But she knew she could do it only if she forgot about Roy. And how he had helped her. And the money she owed him. And her mother's trip to Italy.

Angie left the pit, but Tina stayed there. She could not stop thinking about her problems. Even the fans couldn't make her happy. They kept coming up to her—lots of them. Some even took Polaroid pictures of her and asked her to sign them. It's nice to be famous, Tina thought. But it's not so nice to owe money. And to worry about so many things.

After a while, most of the fans headed back to the stands. Mrs. DeVita came over to Tina and sat down next to her. "You're going to have to race soon," Mrs. DeVita said. "Feeling so low isn't going to help."

"We should have gone back to Highland instead of coming here," said Tina. "I don't like the idea of always trying to beat someone I like. Pop's best friend. Someone who helped me. It doesn't seem fair."

"Look," said Mrs. DeVita. "Racing is the life you want. And it makes me happy to see you get what you want. But remember—if you want to stay in racing, you have to race. No matter who the other drivers are. Roy Cooke will always be our friend. Racing is just his job. It's your job too. So go out and do it."

Tina turned to her mother and gave her a big kiss. "Thanks for saying all that, Mom. I guess you're right." But as Tina smiled at her mother, she wondered if she would ever really enjoy racing again.

Just then, Angie came over to her. "Time to get going," she said. She smiled a big smile. "You're going to win this one, Tina. I know it.

I really feel it will happen. You're going to win."

Tina took her helmet and climbed into the Monza. "Thanks, Angie," she said. But while she put on the helmet, she thought, How can she be so sure?

* * *

The starting lights jumped from yellow to green.

"Hit it," Tina said to herself.

Her car went shooting out from the starting line. So did Roy Cooke's Monza. Wheel to wheel, the two cars roared down the track. The smell of burning tires and smoke, and even the crowd's roar were left behind. Tina hit the finish line in 9.80 seconds, with Roy Cooke right beside her. But Cooke's time was 9.81.

She had done it. It was as easy as that. Tina DeVita had won the Fallnationals in Seattle. She had enough money to pay Roy back. And her mother too. She headed her car toward the pits. But as she did, she saw Cooke driving next to her. Tina felt bad. She couldn't look at him. Think about what Mom said, she told herself. Someone has to win these things. And someone has to lose.

In the pit, Tina's family was all over her even before she could climb out of the Monza. Fans were crowding in.

"Hey, take it easy," she said, pulling her helmet off. She got kisses from her mother, her father, and all of her brothers. Only Angie hung back. As Tina came out from under all the kissing, she saw that Angie looked very pleased with herself. Her eyes were shining—too much, Tina thought. Then it came to her.

"Angie, you didn't—" she began. But she couldn't say the words. "You were in Cooke's pit before the race." She stopped and held her sister's arms. "Did you do something to his car, Angie? Did you?"

Family Matters 6

Angie stood very still. No one in the pit spoke. Tina stood in front of her, just as still. They stared hard at one another.

At last Angie spoke. "What are you saying? That I did something to Roy's car?"

Tina took a hard look at Angie. "Well, you act like you know something that we don't."

"You better take that back," Angie said.

"Take what back? I just asked if you did something. Just say no. Just say you didn't do anything."

Mrs. DeVita stepped in. "You two wait a minute," she said. "I won't have sisters fighting."

"We're not fighting," Angie said.

Everyone in the pit laughed.

"There's nothing to laugh about," Angie said in an angry voice.

"Yes or no?" Tina went on. "Just answer my question. Did you do something to Roy Cooke's car?"

Now Mr. DeVita stepped in between Tina and Angie. He tried to make a joke of the fight. "Come on," he said. "If we're going to have a fight, let's do it right. Tina, you go to that corner. Angie, you get over there."

The fans in the pit laughed again. Even Mrs. DeVita smiled. But neither Angie nor Tina found one thing to smile about.

"Pop," Tina said. "This is between Angie and me. And we don't need a crowd around us, either. Would you people mind leaving?"

"No, I want a crowd," said Angie. "I want to show you up in front of everyone."

For the first time, Tina smiled. "OK," she said. "Show me up. Tell me I'm all wrong. Just say, 'No, I didn't fool around with Roy Cooke's car.'"

"Hey, come on," Timmy said suddenly. "The way you say that, you're telling Angie you believe she could do such a thing."

"That's right," Mark added. "Families should believe in each other."

Then it was Joey's turn to add a word. "Listen," he said. "Tina just wants to know if she won that race fair and square. That's all."

Suddenly Angie started to laugh. "Come on," she said. "This is too much. I'm not going to fight with you anymore. You know me. I get angry one minute, then I forget it the next."

Tina shook her head. "You may want to forget it, Angie. But I don't. Now once and for all, did you or didn't you fool with Roy's car?"

"All right, I'll tell you," Angie said. She tried to make a show out of it. "Everyone step up and listen to the great Angie DeVita."

"May I listen too?"

Everyone turned to see who had spoken. Roy Cooke was standing at the front of the pit. He came into the circle around Angie and Tina. "If you have something to say, I'd like to hear it."

Tina grabbed hold of his arm. "What happened out there, Roy? We were neck and neck, and then all of a sudden you slowed a bit."

"My engine misfired," Cooke said. "And that's what I've come about. Hughes, my mechanic, said he put in fresh spark plugs just before the race. When he checked the car over just now, he found two were cracked.

He swears they couldn't be the same ones he put in."

"You only have his word for it," Angie said right away. "He's probably saying that to save face."

"Hughes wouldn't do that," said Cooke. "But he's doing something else. So if I were you, Angie, I'd get a move on."

Tina broke in. "What's wrong?"

"Hughes is on his way over to the NHRA stand. He said he's going to report you, Angie."

"Report me? What did I do?"

"Hughes said you were hanging around our pit just before the race."

"He's right. I was," said Angie. "I didn't try to hide. I let everyone know I was there. I just wanted to see how your car looked."

"Hughes said you got pretty close to the car," Roy went on.

"Hey, Roy. What are you saying?" It was Mr. DeVita's turn to get mad. "Are you telling us you think Angie put those cracked plugs in your car?"

"No, I don't think she did," said Cooke.

"I'm glad of that," Mr. DeVita said. "So what's the problem?"

"The problem is that my mechanic and I don't think alike," said Cooke.

"Great!" Angie cracked out the word as she started out of the pit. "What you're saying is that Hughes thinks I made you lose the race. Well, I'm on my way to have it out with him right now."

Tina watched, her mouth open, as Angie went storming out of the pit and everyone followed. This fight will probably be wilder than any race, Tina thought. Angie DeVita against Gil Hughes. It would be bad.

"Wait for me," Tina called as she started forward. She was worried about what would happen. But something else was worrying her. Angie had never said those important words. Not once. She had never said, "No, I didn't touch Cooke's car."

Wait a minute, Tina thought. Angie would never do such a thing. No race could be that important to her. As Tina was thinking, she saw that Angie had caught up to Hughes before he reached the NHRA stand. The two mechanics were facing one another in the center of a big crowd.

"You have the wrong person," Angie was saying to Hughes. "If you think someone touched Cooke's car, OK. But don't say it was me. I never put a hand on it. Get that? I never touched it."

Tina saw her mother turn around then. She caught her eye. They both smiled. They believed Angie, and they were happy.

But Hughes was smiling a different kind of smile. "I saw you," he said to Angie.

"You saw me? You're really out of your mind. You're the one who's been doing all the dirty work. I could make a list a quarter-mile long of the tricks you and Roy have pulled. Dirty fuel, missing torque converters, the works. Tina and I have had nothing but trouble lately—thanks to you and your boss."

"Hold on a minute," said Roy Cooke. He stepped forward. "I know you're angry, Angie. But you can't mean what you're saying. Those are fighting words."

Mr. DeVita stepped into the circle then. "Wait, Roy," he said. "Don't you get into this too. The whole thing is getting out of hand."

"I don't like what Angie is saying," Cooke said.

All of a sudden, everyone stopped talking. A voice on the loudspeaker said:

The winners in pro gas class—Tina DeVita in first place, Roy Cooke in second place. Please come up to the stand, Tina and Roy.

Tina threw up her hands. "I can't believe it," she said. "This is really the wrong time for music and prizes."

She went up to Cooke. "Roy, Angie didn't touch your car. I know that, and I'm sure you know it too. But this whole business has turned bad. I want to tell you something. And I want my family to hear it also. Today's race was my last one. This whole thing has done too much to me and to all of us. I don't want to be a part of it anymore. I'll take the winning money and give you what I owe you. And that's that." She turned to her family. "Did you hear what I said? No more racing. Ever."

Angie came over to her. Her face was stiff. "You may not want to race," Angie said. "But I do. I own part of the Monza. So if you don't race it in the World Finals, I will."

CHAPTER 8

Fighting Mad

"I don't like it," said Mrs. DeVita. She put down the book she was reading. Then she picked it up. Then she put it down again. "I don't like it at all," she said.

"What's the matter, Mom?" Tina said as she started to leave for her father's flower shop. She worked there now full-time.

"You're not happy. Angie isn't happy. Your father isn't happy. And I'm not happy."

Tina stopped in the open door. "What are you trying to say, Mom?"

"You stopped driving so we would all be happy," Mrs. DeVita told her. "Do you call this happy?"

"I don't know," Tina said. "But I've paid back all the money I owe. And Angie and I have not had a fight for two weeks. Not since we came back from Seattle."

"I think I like it better when you fight," said Mrs. DeVita.

Tina started out the door again. "Let's forget drag racing once and for all. OK, Mom? Roy Cooke has said he'll buy the Monza after the World Finals. So that's the end of it. The only race I have now is getting to the flower shop on time."

"Go on then," said Mrs. DeVita. "But this isn't the last of it. Angie is getting the car in shape. And you're going to drive it."

Tina laughed as she closed the door. Angie sure takes after Mom, she thought as she smiled to herself. They both think they can win every fight. Well, this is one I'm going to win.

But when Tina came home that night, Angie met her at the door. "Wait until you hear what's happened," she said. She pulled Tina into the living room and sat her down. "Are you ready?"

"Shoot," said Tina. "Only remember—I'm not driving in the World Finals. And you aren't either. The finals are won by points—

the driver's, not the car's. You don't have any points. So you can't even race."

Angie acted as if she didn't hear what Tina was saying. She had a smile on her face, but it was a hard smile. When Tina had finished talking, Angie held out a piece of paper for Tina to see. "Take a look at this," she said.

"It's from World Parcel Service," Tina read. "Oh, the ticket for the torque converter. Let's see the writing. Here it is: 'Angie DeVita.' That sure looks like your writing, doesn't it?"

"Of course it does. Roy Cooke doesn't play games."

"Come on, Angie. Let's not get into that again."

"Roy Cooke knows what my writing looks like, Tina. All he had to do was pay off the driver from World Parcel Service to bring him the converter instead of us. That wouldn't be hard. World Parcel Service does enough business with him. We know that from when we used to hang around his place."

"Roy Cooke wouldn't do something like that," Tina said.

"Sure he would," said Angie. "He wants to win the World Finals as much as you do."

"Look, Angie, this is silly. Anyone could have signed the ticket. Lots of people know your writing," Tina said.

"You're right," Angie told her. Then she sat down in the chair next to Tina. "It doesn't matter if Roy or someone else signed the ticket. The point I'm trying to make is—"

"The point is that we can get the money back from LBH for the torque converter now," Tina said. "All you have to do is tell them that it isn't your writing. You make your *n*'s a different way."

"We'll get the money, all right," said Angie. "But you still don't get the point."

"I believe in Roy Cooke," said Tina. "He's Pop's best friend, and he has been very good to us."

"That may be so. But don't you see, Tina? *Someone* signed that ticket. And got the World Parcel driver to say that it was me. Someone—even if it wasn't Roy—tried to get you to drop out of the race. And it worked. All our other problems could have been accidents. But this ticket shows that someone was out to get us."

"I'm beginning to get mad," said Tina.

"Great," Angie laughed. "That's the best news I've heard all week. Hey, Mom," she shouted all of a sudden. "Come quick! I've got news for you!"

Mrs. DeVita came into the living room. "What's the matter?"

"Something good is the matter," Angie said, still laughing. "Tina is mad!"

"Oh," Mrs. DeVita said. "That's what we've been waiting for."

"No one is going to play with me like that," said Tina. "I don't know who it is. But I won't be beaten. Nothing could keep me out of the World Finals now. *Nothing.*"

"OK," said Angie. "Twenty-four hours a day. Twenty-four hours."

Mrs. DeVita looked at her. "What does that mean?"

"We're going to keep a watch on the Monza," Angie said. "Just to be sure nothing more happens to it before the finals. Everyone but Tina will take turns—24 hours a day."

CHAPTER 9

At the Finals

It was the last day of the NHRA World Finals in California, and the DeVitas were there. Their 24-hour watch had worked fine. Someone in the family had always kept an eye on the car. The Monza was in top shape.

Now the elimination heats were over. It had come down to one last race—a showdown between Tina DeVita and Roy Cooke. The winner would be the best pro gas driver in the world. Everyone in the DeVita family was in the pit, getting ready for the big race.

Suddenly Angie looked up from her work. "Where's Timmy?"

"He was here a minute ago," Tina said.

"Well, he'd better get back here fast," said Angie. "He's supposed to be keeping an eye on the Monza now."

Just then, Timmy walked into the pit, eating a hot dog. Angie came over to him and shouted, "Where have you been?"

"I was just gone for a few minutes," Timmy told her as he bit into the hot dog.

"You were supposed to be watching the car," said Angie. "The race will be starting soon. We're all busy here. We thought you were helping."

"OK," said Timmy, "I'm sorry." He went over to the car and stared at it. "I won't take my eyes off it for a second from now on. You can count on me."

"Thanks a lot," said Angie. "But it wasn't watched for a few minutes, so I better take a look. Someone could have fooled around with it."

She began checking the engine. "I knew it," she said a few seconds later. "I knew it."

Tina and the rest of the DeVitas ran over to the Monza and crowded around the open hood.

"All these people going in and out of the pit," Angie said. "Someone was here all right . . . and did this." She lifted her hand up. Her fingers were covered with something sticky.

Joey made a face. "What's that?"

"Don't ask me," said Angie. "But it's all over the carburetor." She grabbed a rag and wiped her hands. "Now you see what I mean," she said to Timmy. "You turn your back, and there's trouble."

Timmy's face was sad. He asked, "What can I do to make it up?"

"Nothing right now, I'm afraid," Angie answered. "The car needs a new carburetor. And we don't have one."

"Maybe the boys and I can hunt one up," Mr. DeVita said. "Do you think—"

"I was over at Cooke's pit a while ago," Mark broke in. "He has a second carburetor. I saw Gil Hughes holding one in his hand. I thought he was going to change the carburetor that was already in Cooke's car. But he didn't."

Mr. DeVita looked at Angie, then at Tina. "What do you two think? Want me to speak to him?"

"I don't know," Tina told him. "That's asking a lot of Roy. First we tell him he's trying to get me out of the race. Then we take his money. And now we ask him to give us his carburetor."

"He'll do it," said Mr. DeVita. "He wants to run a good race against you, Tina."

Angie hadn't said anything yet. "I'm not so sure about that. Cooke could be setting us up."

"Come on," Mr. DeVita said. "That's too much. This kind of talk is just making us lose time. Mark, let's run over to Cooke's pit and see if he'll let us have the carburetor."

Mark and his father left the DeVita pit right away. In minutes they were back with the carburetor—and with Roy Cooke.

"I'm sorry about what happened to your car," Cooke said to Tina. "I thought I'd come over to see that everything got fixed."

Angie took the carburetor from her brother. She gave Roy Cooke a hard look. "Thanks," she said. Then she began to go over the carburetor inch by inch.

"What are you doing? The race is going to start any minute," Tina said to Angie.

"Just checking," Angie told her. "Stay cool and let me make sure it's all right."

Tina shook her head. "You are really something, Angie!"

"Looks OK to me," Angie said after a minute. She put the new carburetor down and started to get the old one out of the Monza.

At last Angie stood up, holding the old carburetor.

"What a mess," Tina said. "Here's a rag to wipe off your hands."

Angie put down the carburetor and started to clean off her hands. She kept wiping her hands with the rag. But after a few seconds she said, "It won't come off. I'm afraid to touch the new carburetor."

"Let me do it," Roy Cooke said. "I'm an old hand at putting carburetors in." He picked up the part and started fitting it in place.

Angie was about to say something, but she kept her mouth closed. Tina smiled as she saw Angie hold back her words.

Suddenly Mr. DeVita came running up to them. "You both better hurry. They're ready for the final round."

"There's no more time, Roy," Tina said. "Better get back to your car."

"One more second and it will be in place," he said. He wiped his shining face.

"Better let me finish it," Tina said.

But a few seconds later, Cooke had finished the job. "It's all done," he said. "Now we're going to have our race, Tina." He smiled at her. "And may the best driver win."

Then he ran out of the pit.

Angie ran after him. "Hey, Cooke," she called.

Roy Cooke turned around.

"Good luck," Angie said.

CHAPTER 10
Now or Never

What could be keeping him? Tina looked around as she wondered where Roy Cooke could be. She was nosing her Monza toward the warm-up area. But Roy Cooke was not in sight.

Tina thought, Why doesn't he hurry? Doesn't he know this is the most important moment of my life? Then she thought again. Hold it. Maybe it's part of the game. For a second she found herself thinking that maybe Angie had been right. Maybe Roy Cooke wanted so much for her to lose that he had been willing to do anything. Maybe making her lose her cool could be part of it.

Tina felt hot. Her helmet seemed to stick to her head. She wiped a hand across her face.

"Stay cool," she whispered. "This may be just what he wants." Then she got mad at herself. "No, you *know* Roy. He wouldn't try to pull anything. It's thanks to him that you're in the race at all."

Tina had reached the warm-up area when the voice on the loudspeaker spoke.

Roy Cooke to the starting line.

Tina looked toward the pits. Finally she saw Cooke's Monza ride slowly out, and it moved up beside her. She put her hand up to wave to its driver. Cooke turned toward her, but he didn't wave back.

Then the voice on the loudspeaker came on again. It told the waiting crowd about the next two drivers.

Tina DeVita moved through the elimination races this year like an old pro. But as you all know by now, this was only her second year in pro gas drag racing. It's a great story. But the best part of the story is this. Tina DeVita and the man she's racing against now—Roy Cooke—are student and teacher. That doesn't happen often in drag racing. But when it does, look out.

The voice went on, but Tina didn't listen. There was only one thing to think about now. The race that was about to start. Every part of her had to be ready to move out as the yellow lights changed to green. Tina listened to the engine as she started her wheels spinning. The car sounded great. It acted like a well-trained animal. When everything seemed right, she moved slowly toward the starting line. And Roy Cooke moved along right next to her.

At the line, there was a tryout start. Then both cars backed up to the line. Tina fixed her eyes on the yellow lights. She put her hands close around the wheel, her foot on the gas. She didn't know where Tina DeVita ended and the car began. Every inch of her was ready.

She stared at the lights. They were yellow. Then green. *GO!* Gas to the floor, her car went roaring down the quarter-mile course. In less than 10 seconds, it was all over. Tina hit the finish line and braked. Cooke was beside her, braking to a stop.

Even over the engine noise, Tina could hear the crowd roar and the voice coming over the loudspeaker.

*Tina DeVita, 9.75. Winner. Roy Cooke, 9.82.
Second place. Tina DeVita, winner.*

She let out a shout. *Tina DeVita, winner.*
The words rang over and over in her ears.

Back in the pit, the fans crowded around
Tina. They were pushing paper and photo-
graphs at her to sign. Then, at last, Roy Cooke
came walking up to her.

"Hello, winner," he said. He shook Tina's
hand.

Tina smiled at him. "Thanks to you," she
said.

"It was you who did the driving. You're tops, and you know it," Cooke told her.

"I'm only as good as my teacher made me," Tina said.

Just then, Gil Hughes came rushing into the pit.

"I knew you would be here," Hughes said to Cooke. "It looks like you really wanted to lose that race to Tina."

"What are you talking about?" Angie had seen Hughes come in and had headed right for him.

"Wait a minute, Angie," Tina told her. "If Roy tried to lose, it wasn't a fair race. Is that what you're saying, Hughes?"

Hughes didn't answer. Instead, he stared hard at Cooke. "I did everything I could to set up a win for you. And look at how you pay me back."

"What are you getting at?" Cooke looked Hughes in the eye.

"You know as well as I do," said Hughes. "I messed up DeVita's carburetor. And then you went and gave her yours."

"Hold on," Angie said. "You mean you needed that carburetor too?"

Hughes laughed at her. "What do you think? I was going to put a new carburetor in Roy's car. But after I put yours out of business, I knew you couldn't win. So I decided not to change Roy's. Then he goes and gives you the good one. And there wasn't enough time left to do anything about it."

Tina looked at Cooke. "Is that why you were slow coming out of the pits? Because Hughes was trying to work on your old carburetor?"

"I'm afraid so," Cooke said. "But don't look so worried. My carburetor wasn't the reason I lost the race. I lost because you were a better driver. Because you're quick to move, and you know what you're doing. You won the race because you deserved to win it, Tina."

"Thanks, Roy," she said.

Then Angie looked at Hughes. "You were the one, weren't you? All along, you were the one who pulled those tricks."

Hughes didn't answer. He faced Cooke.

"You're slowing down, Cooke. I wanted to help you make it one more time. I wanted to be working for a winner. Now it's too late." He turned around and pushed his way past the people and out of the pit.

For a while, no one said a word. Then Angie spoke up. "I'm sorry," she told Roy Cooke. "I'm sorry I acted the way I did—and thought what I thought."

Cooke smiled again. "Looks as if you had good reason to. You're a fine mechanic, Angie. You just believe in what you do." Then he looked at all the DeVitas as he rubbed his hands together. "Well, let's pick up the pieces," he said. "And why don't we put them together in a new way?"

Mr. DeVita shook his head. "Pieces? What pieces are you talking about?"

Tina looked at Roy Cooke. "I think I know," she said.

"I need a new mechanic," Cooke explained. "And I want the best—Angie DeVita. I've decided to get out of drag racing, but I still want to build racing cars."

"That's what I thought," Tina said.

Cooke laughed. "But there's one thing I bet you haven't thought of. I also need a new driver." He held out his hand. "And I want the best."